INSIDE COLLEGE
FOOTBALL

CLEMSON
TIGERS

BY ROBERT COOPER

SportsZone
An Imprint of Abdo Publishing
abdobooks.com

abdobooks.com

Published by Abdo Publishing, a division of ABDO, PO Box 398166, Minneapolis, Minnesota 55439. Copyright © 2021 by Abdo Consulting Group, Inc. International copyrights reserved in all countries. No part of this book may be reproduced in any form without written permission from the publisher. SportsZone™ is a trademark and logo of Abdo Publishing.

Printed in the United States of America, North Mankato, Minnesota
042020
092020

Cover Photo: Rick Scuteri/AP Images
Interior Photos: Del Mecum/Cal Sports Media/AP Images, 4–5; David Rosenblum/Icon Sportswire/AP Images, 7, 8; Mark LoMoglio/Icon Sportswire/AP Images, 10; Shutterstock Images, 13; Mark Crammer/Anderson Independent-Mail/AP Images, 16; Jake Drake/Cal Sports Media/AP Images, 19; JPK/AP Images, 21, 43; AP Images, 22; John Byrum/Icon Sportswire, 24; Clemson/Collegiate Images/Getty Images, 27; Jerry Wachter/Sports Illustrated/Set Number: X27664 TK1/Getty Images, 30; Phil Coale/AP Images, 32; Craig Jones/Allsport/Getty Images Sport/Getty Images, 35; Jim R. Bounds/AP Images, 37; Doug Buffington/Icon Sportswire/AP Images, 39; Steve Jacobson/IOS/AP Images, 41

Editor: Patrick Donnelly
Series Designer: Nikki Nordby

Library of Congress Control Number: 2019954423

Publisher's Cataloging-in-Publication Data
Names: Cooper, Robert, author.
Title: Clemson Tigers / by Robert Cooper.
Description: Minneapolis, Minnesota : Abdo Publishing, 2021 | Series: Inside college football | Includes online resources and index.
Identifiers: ISBN 9781532192517 (lib. bdg.) | ISBN 9781644944660 (pbk.) | ISBN 9781098210410 (ebook)
Subjects: LCSH: Clemson Tigers (Football team)--Juvenile literature. | Universities and colleges--Athletics--Juvenile literature. | American football--Juvenile literature. | College sports--United States--History--Juvenile literature.
Classification: DDC 796.33263--dc23

TABLE OF CONTENTS

CHAPTER 1
SWEET REVENGE 4

CHAPTER 2
BUILDING DEATH VALLEY 12

CHAPTER 3
HOWARD'S TIGERS 18

CHAPTER 4
FINALLY CHAMPIONS 26

CHAPTER 5
DABO'S DYNASTY 34

TIMELINE	42
QUICK STATS	44
QUOTES AND ANECDOTES	45
GLOSSARY	46
MORE INFORMATION	47
ONLINE RESOURCES	47
INDEX	48
ABOUT THE AUTHOR	48

CHAPTER 1

SWEET REVENGE

The Clemson Tigers faced the Alabama Crimson Tide in the College Football Playoff (CFP) National Championship Game on January 9, 2017. Alabama was looking for its second straight national title—and second straight defeat of Clemson in the championship game. When the Tide jumped out to a 14–0 lead, an Alabama repeat appeared likely.

But Clemson had come from behind to win games before. The Tigers knew they had what it took to stay with Alabama. So they kept working. Eventually that hard work paid off. Two straight touchdowns in the fourth quarter gave Clemson a 28–24 lead with 4:38 to play.

Then Clemson needed a big stop from its defense. The Tide faced a third-and-16 play from their own 26-yard line. Alabama quarterback Jalen Hurts completed a 15-yard pass just short of the

Clemson wide receiver Mike Williams makes a leaping catch against Alabama.

SUCCESS IN LOSS

Deshaun Watson had one of the greatest performances in college football history in a losing effort in the CFP national championship game played in January 2016. Watson's 405 passing yards were the most ever in a national championship game. And with 73 rushing yards, he also broke the record for most total yards in a title game.

first-down marker. If the Tigers could make a stop on fourth-and-1, they would likely run out the clock and win the national championship.

Instead, Alabama running back Damien Harris barreled forward for a first down. Just two plays later, Hurts ran for a 30-yard touchdown, and the Crimson Tide led 31–28.

Just over two minutes remained in the game. For Clemson, it was starting to feel like the previous year's title game, when the Tigers and their star quarterback Deshaun Watson came up just short, losing to Alabama 45–40.

Now Watson had another chance. He'd already put up huge stats. He would end the season with 4,593 passing yards and 41 touchdown passes. He had been a finalist for the Heisman Trophy. But he wanted the national title most of all.

Tigers head coach Dabo Swinney had brought Watson to Clemson. Since taking over as head coach in 2008, Swinney had become known for recruiting elite talent. Watson was one of the top high school quarterbacks in the country. But Swinney could also spot talented players who didn't get as much attention from the scouting services.

✖ **Dabo Swinney, *center*, meets his players to discuss strategy against Alabama.**

One of those players was Hunter Renfrow. The skinny wide receiver was not offered a scholarship by any team in the top division of college football. But Swinney met Renfrow and thought he could play. Swinney, himself a former walk-on receiver at Alabama, offered Renfrow a chance to walk on at Clemson. Renfrow and Watson would play a major role in the end of the game.

Clemson started at its own 32-yard line with 2:01 to go. A field goal would tie the game and likely force overtime. But a touchdown could win it for the Tigers. Watson immediately got to work, moving the Clemson offense down the field.

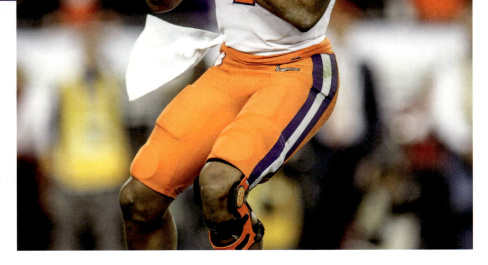

✗ Deshaun Watson took charge on the game's final drive.

On first down, Watson made a 5-yard completion. On second down, he looked to his left and saw wide receiver Mike Williams streaking down the sideline. Watson lofted a high pass, and Williams leaped over the Alabama defender to catch it. Just like that, Clemson was in Alabama territory.

NEW RIVALS

Despite both being premier football programs from the South, Alabama and Clemson had played only 15 times in 116 years before they met in back-to-back CFP national championship games. Clemson had not beaten Alabama since 1905, when it won 25–0 in Columbia, South Carolina. Before their first national championship meeting, the teams had last met in the opening week of the 2008 season, when Alabama won 34–10. Clemson coach Tommy Bowden resigned later that year with Dabo Swinney replacing him. Alabama and Clemson went on to meet in the CFP four years in a row starting after the 2015 season.

Watson completed a short pass on first down, and the clock kept running. He scrambled on second down but could not reach the first-down marker. Clemson had two timeouts left but chose not to use them. The clock ticked down under 30 seconds. Watson hit Renfrow for a six-yard gain to give the Tigers a first down at the Alabama 26.

Clemson was running out of time. Watson spiked the ball to stop the clock with 19 seconds left. The Tigers were in field-goal range. They could play it safe and try to take the game into overtime.

But Watson wanted to end it right then and there. He hit tight end Jordan Leggett for 17 yards to get inside the Alabama 10. The Tigers took a timeout with 14 seconds left on the clock. That was enough time for two or three more plays.

✗ Alabama defensive back Tony Brown (2) can't stop Hunter Renfrow from scoring the game-winning touchdown

They had to be careful to not run out the clock before they could attempt a game-tying field goal in case they couldn't score. On first down from the Alabama 9-yard line, Watson threw for the end zone. Leggett was covered, and Watson overthrew him. That stopped the clock with nine seconds left.

On the next play, Watson looked for Williams. His high pass sailed far out of bounds as Williams went tumbling to the ground. But Alabama was flagged for pass interference. That gave Clemson the ball at the 2-yard line with six seconds to play.

Clemson had to run a quick play. The Tigers would need some time left to kick a field goal if they did not score. Watson took the snap. He rolled to his right. Suddenly, Renfrow broke free of his defender. He ran to the right all alone. Watson spotted him and fired a bullet of a pass. Renfrow caught it as he backpedaled into the end zone. Touchdown! Just one second remained on the clock.

Renfrow's teammates mobbed him in celebration. The Alabama defense looked on in disbelief. It was Renfrow's tenth catch and second touchdown of the game. The former walk-on had just caught the biggest pass in Clemson football history.

The Tigers had won their second national championship and their first since 1981. For longtime fans, it was hard to believe. Clemson was typically a strong program. But under Swinney, the Tigers were competing for national titles year after year.

Swinney had brought a winning attitude and winning players to Clemson, South Carolina. And his Tigers weren't even close to being finished.

CHAPTER 2

BUILDING DEATH VALLEY

Residents of western South Carolina love their Clemson Tigers. That was obvious from the start. They did all they could to build a football program that quickly became a power in the South.

Clemson Agricultural College opened in 1893. The football team began playing just three years later. Thirty students tried out for that first team. Twenty made it. The team won two of its three games that season. College football was a lot different back then. The game looked more like rugby than modern football. The massive stadiums and bright lights were still years away as well.

Before the 1900 season, the school hired an up-and-coming coach named John Heisman. Nobody knew it at the time, but his name would become one of the most famous in college football. Since 1935 the Heisman Trophy has been given out to the best college football player each season.

Tillman Hall is one of the landmarks on the campus of Clemson University.

Heisman coached at Clemson for just four years, from 1900 to 1903. But he had a tremendous impact. The Tigers went 6–0 in 1900 and outscored their opponents 222–10.

But after Heisman left, Clemson entered what has been referred to as the Dark Ages. From 1908 to 1926, the Tigers went 69–82–10 under nine head coaches. In 1921 the school joined the Southern Conference. The 14-team league would eventually include Alabama, South Carolina, Georgia, Georgia Tech, and Auburn.

It was hard to win in the powerful Southern Conference. Financial issues at Clemson made it even tougher. Jess Neely took over as head coach in 1931. The Tigers struggled in his first three seasons. Then he was able to convince the school to put more money into the program. If Clemson was to be a college football force, Neely said, it would need better locker rooms, new equipment, and top facilities that would attract the best players.

Neely slowly began to reestablish the program. The team went just 24–32–5 from when he took over through the first four weeks of the 1937 season. Then Clemson beat South Carolina. Neely went 18–3–2 in his career at Clemson after that. And in 1939, Clemson football once again became a force.

The 1939 season began with a win over Presbyterian. Then the Tigers lost to Tulane 7–6. But they did not lose again that season. They shut out South Carolina 27–0. They defeated Wake Forest 20–7. And they beat Southern Conference foe Furman 14–3. No opponent scored more than seven points against Clemson that year.

That was the first Clemson team to be ranked since the Associated Press (AP) Poll began in 1936. It also was the first to play in a bowl game. The twelfth-ranked Tigers beat No. 11 Boston College in the Cotton Bowl.

Just a few weeks later, Neely left Clemson to take the head coaching job at Rice University. This time, however, the coaching transition was smoother. Frank Howard, an assistant under Neely since 1931, was ready to take over.

Howard led the Tigers to a Southern Conference title in his first year. He went 13–4–1 in his first two years. Clemson was ranked nationally both seasons. Before Howard's third year, the program got a boost as construction of Memorial Stadium began.

Fans should have been buzzing with excitement when the new stadium opened in 1942. However, football took a back seat for a few years after Memorial Stadium was built. The United States fought in World War II from 1941 to 1945. Many young men who might otherwise have been going to college were sent off

PALMETTO BOWL

Clemson and South Carolina first met on November 12, 1896, during the State Fair in Columbia, South Carolina. The Gamecocks won that first game 12–6. The rivalry was suspended from 1903 to 1908 after a near-brawl between students from both schools. Since 1960 the game has alternated between Clemson and Columbia on a yearly basis. For years the game was referred to as the Palmetto Bowl, in honor of the South Carolina state nickname. In 2014 the schools made that name official.

✕ **Memorial Stadium, which is nicknamed "Death Valley," was built in 1942 and now seats 81,500 fans.**

to fight. That had an effect on college and professional sports teams around the country. During wartime the Tigers had three straight losing seasons before going 6–3–1 in 1945.

The tide finally turned for Clemson in 1948. Many remember it as the first great season in Clemson football history. It opened with a 53–0 rout of Presbyterian. Then the Tigers beat North Carolina State and Mississippi State. After that was one of the most famous games in the rivalry with South Carolina. Late in the game, Clemson blocked a punt and returned it for the game-winning touchdown.

HOME SWEET HOME

When Jess Neely became Clemson coach in 1931, he took over a winning program. But the facilities and equipment were old and run down. Even fan interest was low at the time. Neely wanted improvements to help his team compete for conference titles. Yet he thought building a new stadium was a waste of time.

"Don't ever let them talk you into building a big stadium," Neely said as he left for Rice. "Put about 10,000 seats behind the YMCA. That's all you'll ever need."

But Clemson did build a new stadium. Memorial Stadium held roughly 20,000 seats when it opened on September 19, 1942. More than 60,000 seats have been added since then. Entering the 2020 season, Memorial Stadium was the 15th-largest college football stadium in the country. Officially it has 81,500 seats, but many more fans have squeezed in for big games.

Clemson found a way to survive many times that year. The Tigers ended up going 11–0. That included a one-point win over Missouri in the Gator Bowl. The Clemson Tigers were a scrappy bunch who won six games by seven points or fewer.

That also was the year that Memorial Stadium began earning its reputation as an intimidating place for opponents. When speaking with reporters about their upcoming game, Lonnie McMillan, coach of Presbyterian College in Clinton, South Carolina, called the stadium "Death Valley." The nickname stuck. And as Clemson piled up home wins over the years, the name took on a whole new meaning.

CHAPTER 3

HOWARD'S TIGERS

Frank Howard's 1948 team established Clemson as a national power. He coached the Tigers to another undefeated season in 1950. That team went 9–0–1. The tie came against South Carolina. Clemson beat the rest of its regular-season opponents by an average of more than 33 points.

The Tigers earned a berth in the Orange Bowl that year against the Miami Hurricanes. The Orange Bowl was held in Miami's home stadium. Many people in the southern part of Florida looked down on Clemson. They thought it was a lesser opponent. Howard disagreed.

"They ought to read the AP Poll if they want to know about Clemson," he said.

The Tigers were ranked tenth in the nation. The Hurricanes were ranked No. 15. Howard's team backed up its ranking with a

Clemson's mascot, the Tiger, was introduced in 1954 when a student first dressed up as a tiger.

15–14 win. However, the victory happened in an odd way. Miami led 14–13 in the fourth quarter. The Hurricanes then returned a punt for a touchdown, but it was called back because of multiple penalties.

That backed them up to their own 4-yard line. Moments later, Clemson's Sterling Smith broke through the Miami offensive line. He tackled Hurricanes running back Frank Smith in the end zone for a go-ahead safety.

Jess Neely had moved the football program ahead with the Cotton Bowl win after the 1939 season. The Tigers' dramatic victory in the Orange Bowl after the 1950 season helped them take another step forward. It also began the most successful decade in Tigers history up to that point.

Clemson faced Miami again in the Gator Bowl after the 1951 season. This time the Hurricanes came out on top. That was the Tigers' last year in the Southern Conference. After playing one year as an independent, Clemson became a charter member of the Atlantic Coast Conference (ACC) in 1953. The Tigers quickly became one of the new conference's

A ONE-SIDED RIVALRY

The Clemson and Presbyterian football teams met at Clemson to start the season every year from 1930 to 1957. Presbyterian coach Lonnie McMillan feared Memorial Stadium, and he had a good reason for it. He coached his team at "Death Valley" 13 times from 1941 to 1953. In the final 10 visits, his team was outscored 506–33. However, one trip went right for McMillan. In 1943 Presbyterian escaped Memorial Stadium with a 13–12 victory.

✗ Clemson tailback Billy Hair runs around Miami defenders during the Gator Bowl following the 1951 season.

top teams. They won the league title in 1956, 1958, and 1959. Clemson finished the decade with a 9–2 season and a win in the Bluebonnet Bowl.

The 1960s were an odd time for Clemson football. The Tigers ended the 1950s by going to three bowl games in four years. Then they began 1960 as the ninth-ranked team in the country. They boosted that ranking as high as No. 7 during a 3–0 start.

However, a loss at Maryland on October 15, 1960, seemed to trigger a decline. From that point until the end of the decade, Clemson was 47–48–2. And the team never won more than six games or went to a bowl game. But there was one positive. The league was

Clemson coach Frank Howard, *left*, shakes hands with Texas Christian University head coach Abe Martin after Clemson's victory in the 1959 Bluebonnet Bowl.

not very strong at the time. So the Tigers still won ACC titles in 1965, 1966, and 1967.

The program continued to take shape in other ways under Howard. While the Tigers were battling for ACC titles in the middle

HOOTIE'S WAY

Taking over for Frank Howard was not an easy thing to do. Hootie Ingram not only had a 12–21 record in his three years as head coach, but he also nearly put an end to the Run Down the Hill. In 1970 and 1971, Ingram had the team instead dress in the west end and make its entrance there.

The Tigers were 6–9 at home under Ingram. Then they decided to mix things up before a game with South Carolina to close out the 1972 season. They rubbed the rock, ran down the hill, and survived a memorable 7–6 win over their bitter rivals. Ever since that game, the team has entered the field of play by rubbing Howard's Rock and racing down the hill.

of the decade, they also were starting traditions that would become famous throughout college football. One of them established a pregame ritual that became synonymous with the program.

Originally, the team dressed for games at Fike Fieldhouse and then walked to nearby Memorial Stadium. The players entered under a scoreboard in the east end zone. From there, they jogged down a hill and onto the field for their warm-ups.

For years, there was nothing more to it. That was just how they entered the stadium and got ready to play. But one day a fan gave Howard a rock from California's Death Valley that was about the size of a football. A booster club member placed that rock atop the hill in 1966. Soon players began to rub the rock and then dash to the field.

✕ Touching Howard's Rock before a home game remains one of the honored traditions for Clemson players.

The "Run Down the Hill" was first done in 1967 before a win over Wake Forest. Howard used it to motivate his players.

"If you're going to give me 110 percent, you can rub that rock," he told them. "If you're not, keep your filthy hands off it."

The rock became known as Howard's Rock. It paired perfectly with the dash to the field. And a tradition was born.

Between the Death Valley nickname, Howard's Rock, and the Run Down the Hill, Clemson home games had become something special. During Howard's time as coach, the team went undefeated at home 10 times. That only added to the mystique.

The Howard era ended after the 1969 team went 4–6. It was the team's second straight losing season. Three more losing seasons came under new coach Hootie Ingram and another followed under Red Parker. Clemson went 7–4 in 1974, but after winning just five games over the next two seasons, Parker was fired. The program had gone 17 years without a bowl game or a national ranking. The Tigers were in a slump.

Still, there were some quality players in the program when Charley Pell took over as coach in 1977. Among them was quarterback Steve Fuller. He would blossom under Pell and help turn the program back in the right direction.

FULLER AND COMPANY

Quarterback Steve Fuller was one of four Clemson players to achieve All-America status between 1977 and 1979. Offensive lineman Joe Bostic was an All-American in 1977 and 1978. He later played 10 years in the National Football League (NFL). Wide receiver Jerry Butler made the All-America team in 1978. He was Fuller's favorite target. Defensive tackle Jim Stuckey was honored in 1979 when he had 10 sacks.

CHAPTER 4

FINALLY CHAMPIONS

Steve Fuller had started nine games at quarterback for the Tigers in 1976. Under new head coach Charley Pell in 1977, Fuller won the first of two straight ACC Player of the Year Awards. That season, he led the Tigers to an 8–3–1 record and a berth in the Gator Bowl. Pittsburgh crushed Clemson in the bowl game. But at least the Tigers were back on the map.

One of the most famous plays in the history of the Clemson–South Carolina rivalry happened that season. With the Tigers trailing, Fuller hit junior wide receiver Jerry Butler for a last-minute touchdown to claim the win. The twisting 20-yard grab at the goal line ended a thrilling game in dramatic fashion.

Fuller was a senior in 1978. In the Tigers' second game of the season, Georgia shut out Clemson 12–0. But the Tigers came roaring back. They won their next nine games and averaged

Clemson's Perry Tuttle runs the ball against South Carolina. Tuttle played at Clemson from 1978 to 1981.

32.6 points per game. Soon the Tigers were back in the Gator Bowl. Only this time, it was under different circumstances. Pell had accepted an offer to become Florida's head coach, so he did not coach in the bowl game against Ohio State.

Pell recommended assistant head coach Danny Ford as a replacement. So Ford took over before the Gator Bowl. At age 30, Ford was the youngest head coach in Division I football. And his first game was against legendary Ohio State coach Woody Hayes.

NO APOLOGIES

Legendary Ohio State coach Woody Hayes was fired the morning after he punched Clemson's Charlie Bauman. Hayes finished his coaching career with 238 wins—205 of them coming at Ohio State. Hayes never apologized to Bauman. However, he did call Bauman a few months later and congratulated him on the victory.

The Tigers won that Gator Bowl. However, the game is most remembered for one wild moment in the fourth quarter. Ohio State trailed 17–15 with two minutes remaining. The Buckeyes were driving for a potential game-winning score. Then Clemson's Charlie Bauman ended their hopes by intercepting a pass.

On the return, Bauman was knocked out of bounds near Hayes. The Buckeyes' coach then punched Bauman. Hayes had to be restrained by his own players to prevent him from throwing another punch. A brawl broke out. Hayes drew two misconduct penalties, and the game soon ended.

Regardless of the game's controversial finish, Ford had defeated a legend in his first game. After recently suffering through eight losing seasons in nine years, Clemson was back among the country's top programs. It was ranked sixth in the nation when the final AP Poll came out that year. That was the highest ranking in team history.

With an enthusiastic young coach and many talented players, the future looked bright for Clemson. The Tigers went 8–4 in Ford's first full season in 1979. They were invited to the Peach Bowl, where they lost to Baylor.

Despite the defeat, the Tigers could still be proud. They had reached a bowl game in three consecutive years for the first time in school history. And the seniors on that 1979 team had won a school-record 27 games. The 1980s had the potential to be a special time in Clemson, South Carolina.

In 1980 Clemson stumbled a bit, finishing the season just 6–5. The Tigers came into the 1981 season unranked. But Ford was excited about his team's chances. Many top players were returning. Some of them had been around during the stretch of three straight bowl games at the end of the 1970s. Among them were senior linebacker Jeff Davis, senior wide receiver Perry Tuttle, and junior defensive back Terry Kinard. Meanwhile, freshman defensive lineman William "the Refrigerator" Perry soon proved to be a force as well.

Those players helped form a unit that had talent on both sides of the ball. The defense was particularly good. It held each of the team's first seven opponents to 10 points or fewer.

✗ Maryland needed two players to try to stop Clemson defensive lineman William "the Refrigerator" Perry in 1981.

The offense really clicked against Wake Forest in the eighth game of the season. In their 82–24 win, the Tigers set an ACC record for points in a game and a school record with 756 total yards. Clemson followed up that performance with a much closer win

STAR POWER

Jeff Davis, Perry Tuttle, and Terry Kinard were three of five All-Americans on Clemson's 1981 roster. Senior defensive tackle Jeff Bryant and senior offensive tackle Lee Nanney were the others. That team had 23 players who would be all-ACC selections at some point in their careers. A total of 29 players on that championship squad eventually were drafted by NFL teams.

Davis and Kinard are two of the three Clemson players in the College Football Hall of Fame. Banks McFadden, the 1939 football and basketball All-American, is the other. Davis is thought of as one of the great leaders in program history. He had 175 tackles in 1981. In a 1980 game against North Carolina, he recorded an amazing 24 tackles. That was the second-most in a single game in Tigers history. Meanwhile, Kinard finished his career with a school-record 17 interceptions.

at No. 8 North Carolina. Then the Tigers got past Maryland and South Carolina.

Clemson was 11–0 and ranked first in the nation. It only needed to get past Nebraska in the Orange Bowl and the unthinkable would happen—Clemson would be the national champion.

The Tigers' punishing defense let the high-powered Cornhuskers know they were in for a battle. Nebraska went three-and-out on eight of its 12 possessions. The Huskers pulled to within 22–15 late in the fourth quarter. But the Tigers drained most of the remaining clock to seal the win.

Clemson fullback Tracy Johnson flips over the Stanford line in search of the end zone during the 1986 Gator Bowl.

Clemson junior quarterback Homer Jordan was named the game's Most Valuable Player (MVP). He threw a touchdown pass to Tuttle and also ran for 46 yards. That included a 23-yard run to pick up a huge first down with about two minutes remaining.

After the game, Ford was happy to let the rest of the country know a little more about Clemson football.

"We finally proved that there's more to the ACC than basketball," he said. "They didn't believe [in] this team in Las Vegas [where betting odds were made]. Nebraska was favored. They didn't believe [in] this team in Nebraska. Out there the newspapers were asking if we belonged in the big time. Well, you can't brag until you've proved your facts. We've proved it. Now, we can brag."

The Tigers could continue to brag for the next couple of years. They followed up the national title with back-to-back 9–1–1 seasons. They were undefeated in the ACC both years. However, that era of Clemson football was tainted by the discovery of numerous recruiting violations.

Ford capped his career in 1989 with his third straight 10-win season and fourth straight bowl win. At the time, the 1980s had been the best decade in Clemson football history. The 1990s, however, would prove to be more difficult.

NCAA VIOLATIONS

The National Collegiate Athletic Association (NCAA) found 150 rule violations at Clemson from 1977 to the early part of 1982. Clemson's program was placed on probation. The Tigers were banned from bowl games in 1982 and 1983 and barred from national television in 1983 and 1984. The NCAA also cut down on the number of scholarships that the school could give out to incoming players. The Tigers were allowed to keep their 1981 national title. The program was one of many powers to go on probation in a short span, including Georgia, Southern Methodist, and Arizona State.

CHAPTER 5

DABO'S DYNASTY

Danny Ford resigned after the 1989 season after rule violations on his watch were discovered. Ken Hatfield took Ford's place as coach. Hatfield led his first team to a 10–2 record and a win in the Hall of Fame Bowl. It was the fifth straight bowl victory for the program. But the rest of the decade included three losing seasons and one 6–6 finish.

The 6–6 season was in 1999, the first under coach Tommy Bowden. The son of famed Florida State coach Bobby Bowden had coached Tulane to an 11–0 record in 1998 before he took over at Clemson. The Bowden name was well respected in college football. The first meeting between father and son on October 23, 1999, was called "the Bowden Bowl." The attendance of 86,092 still stood as a Memorial Stadium record in 2019. However, the father came out on top as Florida State won 17–14.

Clemson quarterback Woodrow Dantzler passes against the Missouri Tigers during a 2000 game at Memorial Stadium.

The 1980s had featured some of the program's best defensive players of all time. The Tommy Bowden era produced some great offensive stars. First on that list was quarterback Woodrow "Woody" Dantzler. Tommy West, the coach before Bowden, had recruited Dantzler. But Dantzler became a starter in Bowden's first year. He was instantly one of the most dynamic players in school history.

In 2001 Dantzler became the first player in college football history to pass for 2,000 yards and run for 1,000 yards in the same season. The year after he left, fans saw the debut of quarterback Charlie Whitehurst. He left after the 2005 season as the school leader in almost every major passing category.

Bowden went 72–45 in nine-and-a-half seasons at Clemson. He never had a losing season, and he took Clemson to eight bowl games. However, Bowden never won the ACC, and some of his teams fell short of expectations. He resigned six games into the 2008 season. His team was ranked ninth in the nation in the preseason poll but started just 3–3.

Assistant head coach Dabo Swinney was elevated to replace Bowden that year. With a blend of youthful excitement and a love for high-powered offensive football, Swinney quickly had a major impact on the program.

One of the players Swinney recruited while still an assistant was a running back named C. J. Spiller. Spiller gained 1,148 yards from scrimmage and scored 12 touchdowns in his freshman year. By the time he left in 2009, Spiller had gained 7,588 all-purpose yards

✗ Clemson star running back C. J. Spiller runs away from North Carolina State defenders during a 2009 game.

That was the most in school history. His 21 touchdowns in 2009 also were a school record, as were his 51 career touchdowns.

Swinney proved to be an effective recruiter of elite talent, especially at the skill positions. Swinney successfully recruited star wide receivers Sammy Watkins and DeAndre Hopkins. In 2011 Clemson won the ACC for the first time in 20 years and played in the Orange Bowl.

The Tigers won 11 games the next season—the first time since the national title year of 1981. Leading the offense was quarterback

THE FORMER WALK-ON

William "Dabo" Swinney has always had a relentless, positive attitude. Swinney's athletic career took him to Alabama, where he was a walk-on wide receiver. Swinney eventually earned a scholarship, though he rarely saw the field. He caught just seven passes in his Alabama career. Swinney then turned his attention to coaching, starting as a graduate assistant at Alabama and working his way up. After 10 years with the Tide, he moved on to Clemson in 2003.

Tahj Boyd, the ACC Player of the Year. Boyd was the first in a trio of passers who would emerge during the greatest era in Clemson history.

The next one was Deshaun Watson. On his first drive as a Tiger in 2014, Watson threw a touchdown pass. That was merely the beginning. In 2015 Watson led Clemson to a historic season. The Tigers were expected to be good. They were ranked 12th in the nation before the season. But few expected them to end up where they did: in the national championship game.

Watson was a big reason for their success. He passed for more than 4,000 yards and 35 touchdowns. He also ran for more than 1,100 yards and 12 touchdowns. That made him the first player in college football history to pass for 4,000 yards and run for 1,000 yards.

Clemson went undefeated and beat No. 8 North Carolina in the ACC Championship Game. Watson was named the game's MVP. He was then MVP of the Orange Bowl win over Oklahoma that put Clemson in the CFP national title game. Watson was outstanding

Dabo Swinney congratulates Deshaun Watson during the second game of the 2014 season when the freshman quarterback threw three touchdown passes.

again, passing for 405 yards and four touchdowns against Alabama. But the Tigers came up just short, losing a heartbreaker 45–40.

Watson was back and better than ever in 2016. He threw for more yards and touchdowns and got the Tigers back to the title game. This time they got revenge on Alabama, winning their first national title since 1981.

Watson was gone to the NFL the next year. Kelly Bryant stepped in with a fine season at quarterback, but the Tigers fell short of the

ONCE IN A GENERATION

Trevor Lawrence is considered one of the top-rated recruits in history. Standing 6-foot-6 with a strong arm, great mobility, and great intelligence, Lawrence was rated the No. 1 high school player in the nation in 2018. The Georgia native was under heavy pressure to sign with his home-state Georgia Bulldogs, but he chose Clemson. Even before his sophomore season, many NFL draft experts had Lawrence tabbed as a future No. 1 overall pick.

national championship. Clemson ended up with a third straight CFP matchup with Alabama but fell in the semifinal at the Sugar Bowl 24–6.

Bryant's career as a starter lasted just one season. He was ousted by a freshman named Trevor Lawrence, who would go nearly two full seasons without losing a game.

As thrilling as the 2016 season was for Clemson fans, 2018 was likely the best in program history. Clemson rolled through the regular season. The Tigers played only two games in which they won by less than a touchdown. Lawrence threw just four interceptions all season.

Clemson stomped Notre Dame 30–3 in the playoff semifinal. That set up a fourth postseason meeting in a row with Alabama. There was no question who was better this time. Clemson routed Alabama 44–16.

Expectations were high for Clemson in 2019. The Tigers returned most of their key pieces, and Lawrence was expected to contend for the Heisman Trophy. He fell short of winning the award, but Clemson

✕ Trevor Lawrence celebrates a Clemson touchdown against Alabama in the national championship game on January 7, 2019.

still got back to the national title game with another undefeated season. Lawrence was 25–0 as a starter heading into the title game.

A powerful Louisiana State (LSU) team overwhelmed Clemson to end the Tigers' bid for another national championship. But there was no reason to think Clemson's championship run had ended. With Swinney as coach and more talented players on the way, Clemson was living through the greatest era in its history.

TIMELINE

1896 — On October 31, Clemson plays its first football game. The team defeats Furman 14–6 in Greenville, South Carolina.

1921 — Clemson joins the Southern Conference. It is one of 14 teams to make up the new league.

1928 — The Tigers play with new uniforms featuring the brilliant orange for the first time.

1939 — Clemson is ranked nationally for the first time. Banks McFadden is the team's first All-American.

1940 — The Tigers play a bowl b[game] first time, [defeating] Boston Coll[ege] in the Cotto[n Bowl] on January [...]

1940 — On January 11, Frank Howard is named head coach at Clemson.

1942 — Memorial Stadium opens with a 32–13 win over Presbyterian.

1948 — On December 4, the Tigers defeat Citadel to finish the regular season 10–0. They later defeat Missouri in the Gator Bowl to complete an undefeated season.

1953 — On May 8, Clemson joins the ACC. Six other teams are part of the new league.

1956 — Clemson wins its first ACC title and accepts an invitation for the Orange Bowl.

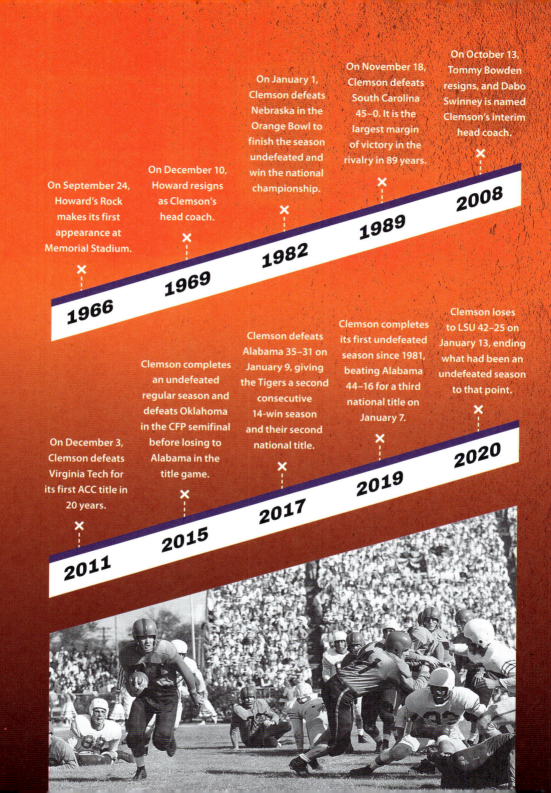

On September 24, Howard's Rock makes its first appearance at Memorial Stadium.

1966

On December 10, Howard resigns as Clemson's head coach.

1969

On January 1, Clemson defeats Nebraska in the Orange Bowl to finish the season undefeated and win the national championship.

1982

On November 18, Clemson defeats South Carolina 45–0. It is the largest margin of victory in the rivalry in 89 years.

1989

On October 13, Tommy Bowden resigns, and Dabo Swinney is named Clemson's interim head coach.

2008

On December 3, Clemson defeats Virginia Tech for its first ACC title in 20 years.

2011

Clemson completes an undefeated regular season and defeats Oklahoma in the CFP semifinal before losing to Alabama in the title game.

2015

Clemson defeats Alabama 35–31 on January 9, giving the Tigers a second consecutive 14-win season and their second national title.

2017

Clemson completes its first undefeated season since 1981, beating Alabama 44–16 for a third national title on January 7.

2019

Clemson loses to LSU 42–25 on January 13, ending what had been an undefeated season to that point.

2020

QUICK STATS

PROGRAM INFO

Clemson Agricultural College
(1896–1963)
Clemson University Tigers (1964–)

NATIONAL CHAMPIONSHIPS

1981, 2016, 2018

OTHER ACHIEVEMENTS

KEY PLAYERS

Vic Beasley (DL, 2011–14)
Jerry Butler (WR, 1975–78)
Fred Cone (RB, 1948–50)
Jeff Davis (LB, 1978–81)
Steve Fuller (QB, 1975–78)
DeAndre Hopkins (WR, 2010–12)
Terry Kinard (DB, 1979–82)
Trevor Lawrence (QB, 2018–)
Banks McFadden (HB, 1937–39)

QUOTES AND ANECDOTES

"This is a game that's not always won by the best football team or by who's supposed to be the best football team. But on that Saturday, you prove who has the best football team. Now, Alabama-Auburn is a great, great rivalry, and they get after it. They have their land-grant jokes; and there's books of 100 Alabama jokes and 100 Auburn jokes—just like it is here. But they let it die about the end of February. The Clemson–South Carolina rivalry, they don't let it die. For 365 days a year there's somebody at every function you go to who's talking about Clemson or South Carolina against each other. It's simply the biggest and best rivalry in football."

—Clemson coach Danny Ford on the rivalry with South Carolina

Dabo Swinney is known for his unique coaching style and the ways he motivates his players. Swinney employs a lot of sayings and catchphrases designed to get his team in the right frame of mind. One of his most famous sayings is "B.Y.O.G.—Bring Your Own Guts." This means that players have to find courage on their own—they can't count on anyone else to do it for them. He also reminds players, "To be an overachiever, be an over-believer," meaning players have to believe in themselves and the team to achieve great things.

William "the Refrigerator" Perry became something of a folk hero after he entered the NFL. As a rookie, he was a key member of the Chicago Bears' dominant defense in 1985. At 335 pounds, he also was used as a blocking back near the goal line and even scored a touchdown in the Super Bowl that season. Perry once was asked what his biggest weakness was. He replied, "Cheeseburgers."

GLOSSARY

All-American
Designation for players chosen as the best amateurs in the country in a particular sport.

bowl game
A game after the season in which teams earn the right to play by having a strong record.

conference
A group of schools that join together to create a league for their sports teams.

rival
An opponent with whom a player or team has a fierce and ongoing competition.

scholarship
Money awarded to a student to p[ay] for education expenses.

spike
In football, intentionally throwing the ball toward the ground to sto[p] the game clock.

walk-on

MORE INFORMATION

BOOKS

St. Sauver, Dennis. *Deshaun Watson: Superstar Quarterback*. Minneapolis, MN: Abdo Publishing, 2020.

Wilner, Barry. *The Story of the College Football National Championship Game*. Minneapolis, MN: Abdo Publishing, 2016.

York, Andy. *Ultimate College Football Road Trip*. Minneapolis, MN: Abdo Publishing, 2019.

ONLINE RESOURCES

To learn more about the Clemson Tigers, please visit **abdobooklinks.com** or scan this QR code. These links are routinely monitored and updated to provide the most current information available.

PLACES TO VISIT

College Football Hall of Fame
cfbhall.com

This hall of fame and museum in Atlanta, Georgia, highlights the greatest players and moments in the history of college football. Among the former Tigers enshrined here are Jeff Davis, Terry Kinard, Banks McFadden, and coach Frank Howard.

Frank Howard Field at Clemson Memorial Stadium
clemsontigers.com/death-valley

The home of the Tigers since 1942, Memorial Stadium is best known as Death Valley for its intimidating atmosphere for visiting teams. The playing surface was named for legendary coach Frank Howard in 1974.

INDEX

Bauman, Charlie, 28
Bostic, Joe, 25
Bowden, Bobby, 34
Bowden, Tommy, 9, 34–36
Boyd, Tahj, 38
Bryant, Jeff, 31
Bryant, Kelly, 39–40
Butler, Jerry, 25, 26

Dantzler, Woodrow "Woody," 36
Davis, Jeff, 29, 31

Ford, Danny, 28–29, 32–33, 34
Fuller, Steve, 25, 26

Harris, Damien, 5
Hatfield, Ken, 34
Hayes, Woody, 28
Heisman, John, 12–14
Hopkins, DeAndre, 37
Howard, Frank, 15, 18, 22–25
Hurts, Jalen, 4

Ingram, Hootie, 23, 25

Jordan, Homer, 32

Kinard, Terry, 29, 31

Lawrence, Trevor, 40–41
Leggett, Jordan, 9–10

McFadden, Banks, 31
McMillan, Lonnie, 17, 20

Nanney, Lee, 31
Neely, Jess, 14–15, 17, 20

Parker, Red, 25
Pell, Charley, 25, 26–28
Perry, William "the Refrigerator," 29

Renfrow, Hunter, 7, 9, 11

Smith, Frank, 20
Smith, Sterling, 20
Spiller, C. J., 36–37
Stuckey, Jim, 25
Swinney, Dabo, 6–7, 9, 11, 36–37, 38, 41

Tuttle, Perry, 29, 31, 32

Watkins, Sammy, 37
Watson, Deshaun, 6–11, 38–39
West, Tommy, 36
Whitehurst, Charlie, 36
Williams, Mike, 8, 11

ABOUT THE AUTHOR

Robert Cooper is a retired law enforcement officer and lifelong football fan. He and his wife live in Seattle near their only son and two grandchildren.